Ashok Rajagopalan's main aim in life is to make people, especially little people, laugh. He has been doing this since 1989, by writing and illustrating picture books, chapter books, comics and magazine pages. He lives in a quiet part of Chennai with his family and books.

Other books in the series:

Gulgul in Jungalu

Gulgul in Parapara

The ADVENTURES of Gulgul

GULGUL IN SEA-SAW GARA

Ashok Rajagopalan

talking CUB
An Imprint of Speaking Tiger Books

TALKING CUB

Published by Speaking Tiger Books LLP
4381/4, Ansari Road, Daryaganj

New Delhi 110002

First published in paperback in Talking Cub
by Speaking Tiger Books in 2020

ISBN: 978-93-89958-97-3

10 9 8 7 6 5 4 3 2 1

Typeset in Crimson Text by Jojy Philip
Printed At: MP Printers (A unit of DB Corp. Ltd.) Noida 201305

To Sudeshna Shome Ghosh,
friend, philosopher and
editor of this series

Gulgul Picks a Place

'Sea-saw Gara!' yelled Gulgul.

Gulgul had picked a nice planet for their holiday that year. The year before, Gulgul and her parents, Jit and Megha, had visited Planet

H4H4H0. They had also been to Planet JUN-84-LU, which Gulgul called 'Jungalu'.

'If you look at JUN, 84 and LU from far away, it reads "JUN-GA-LU",' she said. 'It's easier and faster to call it Jungalu!'

Now she had picked this year's planet. The planet's name was C-54G4R4, but Gulgul called it 'Sea-saw Gara'.

'Because…' she began.

'Right, right,' said her father.

'Because it looks like Sea-saw Gara from a distance.'

'Sea-saw Gara! Sea-saw Gara!' yelled Gulgul.

'Fine, fine,' said Jit. 'Let's go to Sea-saw Gara then.'

'See, Papa,' said Gulgul, 'Sea-saw Gara is half-land and half-sea.'

'Yes, it is,' said Jit.

'Is the land an island then, Papa?' asked Gulgul.

'Right, Gulgul, the land has water on all sides. So it's an island.'

'But the water is a lake, isn't it?'

asked Gulgul again.

'Yes, the water has land on all sides.'

'Then is it an island or a lake?'

'Hmmmmmm,' said Jit, 'Both, I guess. I don't know.'

'It's an island in a lake in an island in a lake in an island in a lake in an island...'

'Megha, help me!' said Jit. 'Take her away!'

'Come, help with the packing, dear,' said Gulgul's mother, Megha.

'But I want to help Papa with the planning, Mamma.'

'Packing first,' said Megha, firmly, as she led Gulgul away.

'Wall, open Maps and show me the shortest route to C-54G4R4,' said Jit to the TV wall.

'Opening Maps,' said the TV wall.

'Not fair! Fathers have all the fun!' grumbled Gulgul.

The TV wall told Jit all about C-54G4R4 and how to get there.

C-54G4R4 was about two days away from planet GR33N, their home planet. It had a big water park. It had the usual water park rides: wave pools, splash castles and slip slides. It also had scuba diving, snorkelling and submarine safaris. If you go on a submarine safari, you get to see animals that you will never see anywhere else! Animals that lived only on that planet. Gulgul looked forward to meeting these strange animals.

'Is our space-car ready, Mama?'

she asked, stuffing a small box with towels, hankies and socks.

'No, dear,' said Megha. 'Some parts haven't come yet. I need a gimbal and some ballutes.'

'Whatever,' said Gulgul. 'When then? Now how will we go?'

'Don't worry, dear. Cabs go to that planet. We are taking a cab this time.'

'Can we take Paru with us this time?'

'Ask Papa,' said Mamma.

Paru was Gulgul's pet, a robot parrot.

'Can we take Paru with us, Papa?' asked Gulgul. 'We left her at home last time.'

'Please don't say "can",' said Jit. 'Say "may".'

'May we take Paru along?' asked Gulgul.

'Please say "please",' said Jit. 'You should learn to be polite.'

'Okay, Papa,' sighed Gulgul. 'Please may we take Paru along?'

'No,' said Jit, 'She is safer here. You keep losing the toys you take outside. So, no!'

'Paru! Come here,' called Gulgul.

Paru flew over to Gulgul's shoulder.

'Go ask Papa if you can come with us,' said Gulgul.

'Okay dokey, Gully gully!' said Paru, and flew away.

'Papa papaya,' said Paru to Jit, 'Please may poor Paru come with you? Please, please?'

Jit could not say, 'no', to such a polite request.

'Okay, you may. But don't go

flying off too far. Stay close to us all the time.'

'Okay dokey, Papaya,' said Paru.

'And don't call me Papaya,' said Jit.

'Yay!' said Gulgul. 'Papa said yes!'

'Then pack Paru's spare battery and charger, too,' said Megha. Moms think of everything.

The next morning, they were ready to go. Gulgul kept jumping up and down.

'Sea-saw Gara! Sea-saw Gara! Gulgul's going to Sea-saw Gara!' she yelled.

'Sea-saw Gara!' said Paru. 'Ghee Gaw Sarah!'

'Silence! Somebody take these brats away!' said Jit. 'I am trying to book a space-cab here!'

'Hush, dears,' said Megha. 'Silence, now, please.'

The Submarine Safari

Finally, the space-cab was booked. It landed on their terrace a few minutes later.

'C-54G4R4, ma'am?' asked the pilot.

'Yes, please drop us there,' said Megha.

'Sea-saw Gara,' said Paru.

'Huh?' asked the pilot.

'We call it Sea-saw Gara,' said Gulgul, 'because it reads like that from far.'

'That's a good idea! You are a clever girl,' said the pilot, 'Easy to say and remember! Okay, let's go. Please wear your seat belts now.'

Zoooooooooom! They were off!

'Yay!' said Gulgul on seeing the BIG water park for the first time.

'Whee!' she

screamed as she slid down the long slide.

'Ooooooh!' she said as she dropped into the pool with a big splash.

All day, she had fun, more fun, and still more fun. The family returned to their hotel rooms in the evening. Tired and sleepy, Gulgul went to bed early.

'What are we doing today?' she asked, bouncing out of bed the next morning.

'A submarine safari,' said her mother. 'The submarine has glass walls for…'

'For us to see corals and fish and everything!' said Gulgul.

'This planet is home to many plants and animals that can't be seen anywhere else in the universe,' said Megha.

'Yay!' said Gulgul. 'I can't wait!'

The glass submarine was ready

and waiting when they arrived at the dock.

'They say that it is built of the strongest glass in the world,' Megha told them.

'It is a beauty!' Gulgul was jumping up and down.

'Come, let's join the queue,' said Jit, pointing at a line of people waiting to board the submarine. The line was actually just a family. A family of four: parents and two little boys of the same size.

'Twins!' said Gulgul, 'See, they are

same-to-same!'

'Hush, dear,' said Megha.

'They are twins,' said their mother proudly. 'Dev and Anand, say "How do you do."'

'My name is Dev,' said one boy, 'How do...'

'You do?' said his twin, 'My name is Anand.'

'Hi, hi!' Gulgul replied. 'I am Gulgul.'

'We are Diya and Yadi,' said the mother of the twins. 'We are from B33.'

'That's the moon of...' began Dev.

'...the planet HON3Y!' finished Anand.

Two people smartly dressed in white uniforms stood near the hatch of the submarine to welcome them.

'Welcome aboard,' said one. 'I am Captain Piya, Chief Pilot.'

'Hello!' said the other. 'I am Peter, Co-pilot. This is the first trip of the submarine, and you are the first passengers to take this safari.'

'What? First trip? This is bad news,' said Jit. 'It's not safe to take the first trip! Let's go back!'

'Who asked you to tell them that, Peter?' Piya frowned at the Co-pilot. 'Don't worry, sir. We will take care of everything. We have been trained well.'

'Don't worry, Jit,' said Megha, 'I am sure they took care of everything.'

'We are the first,' Gulgul was jumping up and down again. 'We are the first!'

The line of people went into the submarine and took their seats. Peter sat at the front. He pressed several buttons and pushed a lever down.

BRRRRRRR...

'Careful,' warned Captain Piya, 'Not so fast!'

BRRR...OOOOOOOOOSH! The submarine swam forward. Then it dived.

'Look, Paru!' Gulgul cried. 'We are going down! The water is going up!'

'Down, down, up, up,' said Paru.

Everybody went 'Ooh!' and 'Aah!' as the glass ship went deeper and deeper, until it almost touched the bottom of the sea. Then the submarine slowed down and swam gently in the water.

'You may leave your seats, now,' said Piya. 'Please feel free to stand near the walls and look at the wonders of our underwater scenery.'

Sea Monster

Blue sunlight shone through the surface. It glittered on corals and sea flowers of many colours. Here and there swam schools of fish, big and small, short and long. Some fish had spots, others had stripes. Some were glassy, like the submarine. Gulgul could see right through those fish. These little fish swam over to look at the people behind the walls.

'Little fish see big fish,' said Paru.

'They must think that we have been swallowed by a giant glass-fish, Paru!' giggled Gulgul.

She took out her camera.

'Smile, little fish,' she said.

Meanwhile, there was trouble at the front, or prow, of the submarine.

'Maps, show direction,' commanded Peter.

'Go straight for 10 yards, and then turn to your right,' said the Map Monitor. Then it went BEEP!

'Why is it beeping?' asked Piya.

'Maps? Are you there?' said Peter.

BEEP!

'I turned to the right. Now, how do we go, Maps?' asked Peter.

Maps beeped again, and then said, 'Sorry, I am not connected.'

'She doesn't sound sorry at all,' Piya frowned at Maps.

'Now what do we do?' asked Peter. 'We have come too far! Maps has lost its signal! We don't know where we are, and where to go!'

'Don't shout, Peter,' whispered Piya. 'You will scare our passengers.'

'Okay, Captain,' Peter whispered back. 'But where do we go?'

Captain Piya pointed to the clock.

'Let's go straight for a while, for

thirty minutes, and then return to dock. We may get connected again.'

'Okay, Captain!'

'Okey dokey, Cappy Tappy!' said a voice behind them. It was Paru!

Paru flew to Gulgul's shoulder and pecked at Gulgul's ear.

'Ow!' said Gulgul, who had been busy looking at multicoloured jelly fish. 'What do you want, Paru?'

'We are lost, Gully gully!'

'Lost? What do you mean, "lost"?'

'Maps went whaps!'

'We are lost!' yelled Gulgul.

'Not last,' said Jit. 'We are the first. That's bad, I think.'

'Lost, Papa, lost!' said Gulgul. 'The pilots have lost direction!'

'What?' yelled Jit.

Everybody began shouting and screaming.

'We are lost!' yelled Dev and Anand.

'Help!' screamed Yadi and Diya.

'Call somebody!' said Jit.

'Where's the Captain?' asked Megha.

'Help!' screamed the parents of the twins again.

Captain Piya tried to calm everyone down.

'Listen, people!' she said. 'We are not lost. We will just return to the dock, taking the same route back. Don't worry.'

That calmed everyone down a little.

The passengers seemed worried, but they worried in silence.

'Captain,' whispered Peter after a while, 'this is not the same route we took.'

'This is not the same route,' Megha told Jit. 'Look at those seaweeds! I don't remember seeing them before.'

Giant seaweeds of an orange colour waved wildly in the water.

'I told you we should not have taken this trip,' said Jit. 'I told you it wasn't safe!'

'Yes, dear,' said Megha.

The pilots steered the submarine carefully through the seaweed.

'Go right! Now left!' Piya was telling Peter. 'Straight! Turn, turn, turn! Not left, you…Right, right!'

'Right, Captain,' said Peter, sweating heavily, turning the steering wheel this way and that.

'Monster!' yelled Jit suddenly. 'Sea Monster!'

Diya and Yadi screamed.

A long and spotted arm pushed through the strands of seaweed.

'Straight ahead!' shouted Piya.

'Okay, Captain,' said Peter.

Gulgul did not scream. She smiled.

'Uncle Hatch has come here to save us again,' she said.

'Uncle Hatch?' asked Dev.

'Who's that?' asked Anand.

'Hatch Patch,' Paru told everyone.

'A kind friend with a long and spotted trunk,' explained Gulgul.

'We met him in Jungalu. No, it's not Uncle Hatch!'

'It can't be Hatch Patch, dear,' said Megha. 'There's no way he would leave his home planet.'

She was right. It was not a spotted elephant that came out of the seaweed.

'It is really a sea monster!' said Jit, and everybody screamed.

'Help!'

'Giant octopus! Help!'

Triopus

The big creature had only three tentacles. With these it tried to grab the submarine.

'Full speed ahead!' yelled Piya. Peter pulled levers and pushed buttons. The submarine leaped forward, throwing the passengers off their feet. BRRRROOOOOOSH!

The passengers rolled back to their seats.

'An octopus,' said Dev.

'With three arms only,' added Anand.

'Octo means eight. This is a triopus,' said Gulgul. 'Look! It's attacking us again!' The triopus made another grab at their ship.

'Faster!' yelled Piya. Poor Peter pulled hard at the lever.

'I can't go any faster, Captain!'

'Turn left! Go through the seaweed,' said

Piya. 'The creature won't be able to see us then.'

The submarine sailed through the weed but stopped soon.

'The grass is too thick here, Captain,' said Peter. 'Can't go any further.'

'Seaweed, not grass. The sea monster's gone. Let's back out of the weeds now.'

Peter pushed the lever.

BRRRRRRRRRRR...OOOSH BRRRRRRRRRR BRRRRRRR... OOOSH. Brrrrr.

'Stuck!' yelled Peter. 'We are stuck in the seaweed!'

'Shut up, Peter! Calm down! Don't shout!' screamed Piya.

'We are stuck,' whispered Peter.

'Sea monster strikes again,' yelled Jit. The triopus had seen them.

It reached through the weeds and grabbed the submarine with its three tentacles.

'Help!' screamed everybody.

'Look,' said Jit. 'More monsters!' Two more had appeared above them.

'This one has four arms,' Dev pointed at one.

'That one has five,' Anand pointed at the other.

'These are not triopuses,' said Gulgul. 'What do we call them, Mamma?'

'Hmm,' said Megha. 'You may call the four-armed one a quadropus. The five-armed one is a pentopus.'

'Triopus, Quadropus, Pentopus,' said Paru happily.

'This is no time to name the monsters,' shouted Jit. 'We are going to be eaten alive by them, four-armed or five. We will become their breakfast!'

Dev and Anand's parents fainted in shock.

'Not breakfast, Papa,' said Gulgul, looking at the clock. 'It's nearly lunchtime.'

The three sea animals wrapped their tentacles around the submarine. BLOOOORP! They pulled it off the seaweed.

'Captain,' said Peter. 'What do we do?'

'Everybody, wear your seat belts, please!' said the captain.

The three sea animals pulled the

ship to the surface. Then they dashed through the waves at top speed, taking the glass submarine with them. The pilots and passengers inside could only watch helplessly as they went on this no-fun ride.

'They must be hungry,' said Jit. 'They are in a big hurry to have us for lunch.'

'Hey, look!' said Peter. 'They are taking us to their home.'

They were being taken to what looked like a big rock floating in the distance. As the rock came closer, they could see that it was, in fact, a small island. An island with buildings of all shapes and sizes on it. And streets and parks and fountains.

'They are taking us to a civilized place,' said Megha. 'I don't think we need to worry.'

'Yes, Papa,' Gulgul smiled. 'They won't eat people if they are so civilized.'

Dev and Anand's parents woke up and smiled hopefully.

'That's right,' said Diya.

'Whew!' breathed Yadi.

'Nonsense, Gulgul,' said Jit, 'Don't civilized people eat squids and other sea animals? Why can't sea animals eat humans?'

Dev and Anand's parents stopped smiling.

Soon, the submarine was dropped on land.

'Should we go outside, Captain?' asked Peter.

'I think it's safer to wait and see,' was the reply.

They waited and watched as the three sea animals released the submarine and crawled up the beach. More animals gathered at the beach. The smaller ones had only three or four tentacles, but Gulgul noticed that the bigger ones had more. Some had six and two had seven arms. The bigger they were, the more arms they had. The biggest and oldest giant of them all was an octopus, with eight tentacles.

The octopus crawled slowly towards the submarine. He then

waved at the people inside it. The people inside did not wave back. They only stared at the octopus.

The octopus knocked gently on the top of the submarine.

'Does he wish to come in?' asked Jit. 'Don't let him!'

Octopus City

'I guess he wants us to come out, dear,' said Megha. 'Captain, let's open the hatch and go outside. They seem friendly.'

'Shouldn't we wait?' asked Yadi.

'Let's go with them, Yadi,' said Diya. 'Megha is right. They seem friendly.'

Piya asked Peter to open the hatch. Peter opened the hatch and led the passengers out in a line. Yadi was the last in line.

As soon as they trooped out, the giant octopus raised an arm in greeting.

'Good day, Humans!' he said. 'Welcome to Octopus City, Turtlepura!'

'Good day to you,' said Captain Piya. 'Thank you. I am Captain Piya.'

'I am Peter, Co-pilot,' said Peter.

'I am Chief Ashtakara,' said the octopus, after all the passengers had told him their names. 'We are happy to have you here. This island always gives a big welcome to those who lose their way. You may wish to thank Thom, Dhik and Aari, who rescued you.'

'They were the reason we needed rescuing,' muttered Jit.

'Thank you, Thom, Dhik and Aari,' chorused everyone else.

Ashtakara took them through the main road and into the city. Octopuses of various sizes and number of arms gathered in the streets to greet them.

'Thom is thirty years old,' explained Ashtakara. 'We grow a new arm every ten years till we are eighty. No more after that.'

'So Dhik is forty and Aari fifty?' asked Gulgul.

'Yes, you are right and a clever girl,' said the chief.

Gulgul and her parents smiled proudly at that.

'This is Octopus City...' said Gulgul to her mother as they followed the chief into the city.

'Yes, dear,' said Megha. 'But why is this Turtlepura? Where are the sea turtles?' asked Gulgul.

'I am sure they will be around somewhere.'

Ashtakara heard that and laughed heartily.

'Sure you will see turtles,' he chuckled. 'At least one. Wait and see, ha ha ha, wait and see.'

'What's the joke?' muttered Gulgul, crossly.

'Wait and see turtle,' said Paru.

The octopuses lived in big glass houses, most of the rooms filled with seawater.

'They look like big aquariums,' laughed Gulgul.

'Why do you laugh? What's the joke?' asked Ashtakara. 'We do call our houses aquariums.'

'Right,' said Aari.

The humans were invited to stay in a big aquarium near the beach.

'Please stay with us as long as you wish,' said Chief Ashtakara, leading them to the dining room. 'We have prepared a feast for you, honoured guests. Here are sea-fruits, sea vegetables and sea-nuts.'

Everybody sat down to eat.

'We don't grow anything on land,' said the chief. 'All food is grown in the sea.'

'Right!' said Aari, serving them bowls of water. 'Most of us work as underwater farmers.'

'Do you like our food, guests?' asked the chief, as Dhik brought forward a big vessel of brown sea-grass.

'Yes, thank you, Chief,' said Gulgul,

biting into a ripe sea-apple. 'I love the fruit and nuts. They taste great. The vegetables are okay, I guess. But I don't want any of that grass, please!'

'I don't want it too,' said Jit.

'Oh, that's our most important delicacy,' said the chief. 'We always have brown grass for dessert.'

'Don't be rude, dears,' said Megha. 'Have a little grass. It's only polite to taste their most important delicacy.'

Jit obediently chewed on a bunch of grass. Gulgul did not. She did not want to ruin the taste of all the goodies she had just eaten.

'Help! Water!' yelled Jit suddenly, through a mouthful of munched grass. Megha pushed a bowl of water into his hands.

He gulped down the water but spat it out immediately.

'Yuck! Salt water!'

'Yes,' said Aari. 'Best seawater to drink.' Gulgul was glad that she had tasted neither the grass nor the water.

'Thank you, Aari,' said Megha, 'humans can't drink seawater. Gulgul, fetch our water bottles from the submarine. Hurry, please.'

'We will come with you,' Piya rose from her seat. 'We have finished our lunch. We need water, too, and we need to check the submarine for damage and do repairs.'

'If needed,' laughed Peter.

Water Problem

'We can't stay here long,' said Captain Piya later. 'We are running out of drinking water. We have only three cans of water left. And those will be finished by dinner.'

'But our phones and maps are not connected,' Peter pointed out.

'We can't stay here without water,' said Piya. 'We HAVE to leave.'

'Oh what will we do?' asked Diya.

'What will we drink?' asked Yadi.

'We can explore the island to see if there are ponds or lakes here,' said Megha. 'Coming, dears?'

'I have to help the captain repair our ship,' said Peter. 'Sorry.'

'By "dears", I meant my daughter and husband,' said Megha.

'And parrot,' said Paru.

'Let's go repair our ship, Peter,' said Piya.

'Okay, dear…I mean, Captain.'

'Let's wear our helmets,' said Megha, as they stepped out. 'Looks like rain.'

She was right. The sky was filled with dark, grey and fat clouds. Here and there, amidst the clouds, flashed lightning.

'While we look for ponds, let's also look for turtles,' said Gulgul.

'See turtles,' said Paru.

'Hopefully,' said Megha.

They soon left the city and walked far inland.

'No trees, no ponds, and no lakes,' grumbled Jit, after they had explored most of the island.

'Yes, dear,' said Megha. 'Just sand, rocks and weeds. Never seen an island like this in my life.'

'At least let's look for turtles, Mamma,' said Gulgul.

'Okay, Gulgul, we can take the beach route back. It may take a little longer that way, though.'

The three walked and walked but saw no turtles. Gulgul frowned.

'They shouldn't have named the island Turtlepura!' she kicked at the sand.

'Hey, look! Sea horses!' shouted Jit.

In the sea, riding the waves was a fleet of five animals that were half horse and half fish. They leapt over

the waves, and turned somersaults in the air.

'They are striped, Papa,' said Gulgul. 'They are not sea horses. They are seabras!'

All at once the five creatures stopped playing about and swam away at great speed, neighing in fear.

'What's happening?' asked Gulgul.

'There, dear,' said Megha. 'They are being chased by…'

'Merlions!' yelled Jit. The seabras were being chased by a pair of ferocious animals, half-lion and half-fish.

'Yay!' roared the merlions, swimming after the seabras.

'Neigh!' cried the seabras, speeding away.

'Hope the seabras swim faster than the merlions,' said Gulgul.

'Merlions have to eat, too, dear,' said Megha.

A drop of water plopped on Gulgul's nose.

'It's raining!' laughed Gulgul. 'Yay!'

'Let's hurry back,' said Jit.

'Aw, Papa,' said Gulgul. 'I love the rain.'

'We had no luck,' said Jit to Captain Piya.

'That's bad news! We have to leave immediately,' said Piya. 'We don't have enough water.'

'Where is Gulgul?' asked Dev. 'We are going swimming.'

'Our living room is a swimming room. It's filled with water,' said Anand.

'Gulgul and her mother have gone to see the chief about something,' said Jit.

'I hope they are back soon,' said Piya. 'We may have to leave after dinner.'

'Though we don't know the way,' muttered Peter.

'Shut up, Peter,' said Piya.

Gulgul and Megha arrived with good news and three tubs of fresh water. The tubs were brought in by Thom, Dhik and Aari.

'With the chief's help, we managed to get some water,' said Megha.

'Rainwater!' explained Gulgul. 'They gave us three big funnels and three tubs to collect rainwater.'

'What a relief,' said Yadi. Diya hugged Gulgul.

'It was Gulgul's idea to collect rainwater,' announced Megha proudly.

'They say that it rains here every day, and quite heavily,' said Gulgul.

'Everybody clap hands for Gulgul,' ordered Captain Piya. Everybody clapped hands.

'Three cheers!' screamed Dev.

'For Gulgul!' shouted Anand, and everybody hip, hip, hurrahed Gulgul.

'Thank you,' said Gulgul. 'Now we can stay here as long as needed.'

'At least till they send

someone to take us back to the water park,' said Piya.

Turtle, finally!

Gulgul loved their rooms. The bedroom was dry, but the living room was filled with water. She had fun swimming in it whenever she wanted to. She could have a bath on the roof whenever it rained, too.

'I love Turtlepura,' she told her mother the next morning at breakfast. 'But I would love to see some turtles before we leave.'

'You will, today, surely,' said Thom, serving them sea-nuts. 'Right, Dhik?'

'Sure you will, Gulgul,' nodded Dhik.

'Really? Yay!' said Gulgul.

'The chief wishes to meet you two after breakfast,' Aari told Captain Piya and Peter.

'I have finished eating,' said Piya.

'Will go and see him right away. Come, Peter.' They left.

'Some grass, Gulgul?' asked Thom.

'No, thank you, Thom.'

The captain and co-pilot returned shortly. They were panting and puffing, because they had run all the way from the chief's house.

'Danger!' puffed Piya.

'Beware!' panted Peter.

'What? What? What?' asked Dev and Anand's parents.

DING DONG! DING DONG! DING DONG!

The noise boomed through the room and shook the plates and vessels on the table.

'That's the warning bell!' said Piya.

'The first warning!' said Peter.

'What warning? Why bell?' asked Jit. 'How? Where?'

Piya let out a long breath before replying.

'The island is going to sink!'

'Sink?' asked Jit.

'Sink!' said Yadi.

'Yes, sink!' said Peter. 'That's the

first warning bell. The island sinks once a week on a day they call Downday, and today's Downday!'

'Come outside and look! Come,' said Piya. Peter and the passengers followed her outside.

The octopuses in the streets were crawling home.

'See you later, people!' said Thom, as he left with Dhik and Aari.

'Later, sea people,' said Paru.

'See?' asked Piya. 'Everybody goes into their homes and stays there. Then the island sinks and remains underwater for two days. Then it comes up again, on Upday.'

'Now, let's hurry!' said Peter.

'Hurry where?' asked Jit.

'To the submarine,' said Piya. 'We have an hour till the next bell rings. Hurry, hurry!'

They hurried. Jit and Megha began packing their bags.

'Yadi!' said Diya. 'Go get the kids. They are living in our swimming room!'

'You mean, swimming in the living room.'

'Go, go, go!' yelled Diya.

DING DING DING DING DING! DING DONG, DING DONG!

'Second bell!' said Gulgul.

'Hurry, hurry,' said Paru.

'Look,' said Gulgul. The sea seemed to be slowly swallowing the beach. The beach became smaller and smaller, till it disappeared completely. Now the sea had reached the streets. The passengers ran to the submarine, which the pilots had managed to bring closer to the main road. They quickly dashed into the ship and took their seats. They sat in their seats and watched as the island sank. The octopuses waved at them from their aquariums. Gulgul waved back.

'There's Thom, Dhik and Aari,' she waved her arm wildly.

The water covered the streets and waves dashed against the glass walls of the aquariums. Slowly the buildings sank with the octopuses inside them.

B A R R R R R R O M! BROOOOOOOOOSH! The submarine dived into the water.

'Weird! But why does the island go up and down like this?' asked Gulgul. 'Why doesn't it just stay up there like any good island?'

'You will soon see why,' said Piya, as the submarine dived deeper.

'We are under the island now,' said Peter. Sure enough, when Gulgul gazed upwards through the glass walls, she could see the smooth bottom of the island.

'What are those long rocks at the sides? They seem to be moving. They look like big arms and legs…oh!' Gulgul's eyes widened in wonder.

At one end of the island was a gigantic head. The head of a giant…

'Turtle!' yelled Gulgul.

'Right,' said Piya. 'The whole island is a giant turtle. That's why it's called Turtlepura. She goes into the water now and then. Chief Ashtakara said that the turtle stays underwater for a whole month in summer.'

'Wow!' said

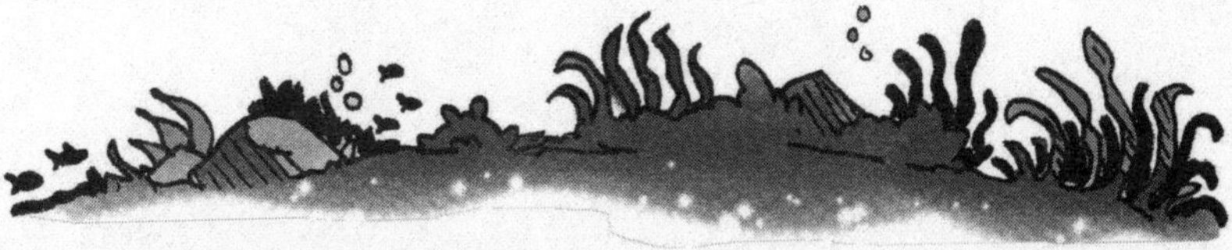

Gulgul. 'I saw a turtle, finally! A big, big one! Now I know what they meant when they joked that I will get to see a turtle.'

'See turtle?' asked Paru.

'Where's my camera?' Gulgul started taking pictures of the giant turtle.

Attack of the Merlions

'Let's keep going straight ahead, Peter,' ordered Piya. 'We will reach land sometime.'

'Okay, Captain.'

'She's right,' said Dev.

'Yes, this planet is a big lake with land on all sides,' said Anand.

'No, no, this planet is a big island with water on all sides,' said Peter.

'This is an island on a lake in an island on a lake in an island...' said Gulgul.

'Silence, everybody! Shut up Peter!' yelled Piya.

'We are sailing in a straight line till we reach land,' Gulgul told Megha. 'Guess that's a good idea.'

'Yes, that's the best we can do.'

'Look, those weeds again!' said Jit.

Everybody ran to take a look at the giant orange seaweed.

'This is where we got stuck,' said Peter.

'Take the ship above the weeds, Peter,' said Piya.

'I am trying, Captain,' Peter pulled the lever up.

'Also, keep checking to see if we are connected,' said Piya.

'Maps, are you there?' asked Peter.

'Sorry, I am not connected,' replied Maps.

'No use being sorry, you stupid Map! Get connected! Keep going straight ahead, Peter,' said Piya. 'At full speed!'

Peter increased the speed of the submarine. He steered it through the weeds.

BRRRRRRRR OOOOOOOOSH! OOOSH! Ooosh!

'What happened, Peter? asked Piya.

'We are stuck in the sand!'

Peter pushed and pulled the lever, but the submarine stayed put. It even sunk into the sand a bit more.

'Its weight is pulling it into the loose sand,' said Peter.

'Suppose we make the submarine lighter?' asked Megha.

'How do we do that?' asked Piya.

'We can all get out of the thing,' said Gulgul. 'But then, the water will rush into the submarine, won't it?'

'No fear,' said Piya. 'We have a special door on the side. It is

actually a triple door with three chambers. Water will not get in.'

'Yay!' said Gulgul.

'Do we have enough diving suits and helmets?' asked Megha.

'Sure, there's a set under each seat,' said Peter.

'Then let's get out now,' said Megha.

Jit and the parents of Dev and Anand did not like wearing the suits and stepping out. But the children were delighted! Gulgul took her camera along and began taking pictures of the underwater scenery. Paru swam out with them. Air or water, it was the same to her.

Peter, who remained inside, pushed the lever again.

BRRRRRRRRRRRR.

'No use,' he thought. 'It's still stuck in the mud.'

Everybody was worried now. They looked at Piya. But the

captain did not know what to do. Diya and Yadi tried pushing the submarine loose. Piya, Megha and Jit joined them. But the submarine did not budge a bit.

Suddenly, Peter began waving his arms. He made all kinds of faces. He jumped up and down. He ran to the special door and yelled, 'Come in! Come in quick!'

Everybody stared at him. Piya scratched the top of her helmet worriedly. What had happened to the co-pilot?

Peter pointed at the weeds behind them and made a fierce face.

Gulgul turned around and screamed inside her helmet.

A scary face glared at her from the weeds. Half lion and half fish—a merlion! She looked again. More such beasts behind the rocks! Four more! They did not look friendly at all.

Everybody screamed inside their helmets. Jit grabbed Gulgul's and Megha's arms and tried to run. He stumbled. Then he remembered that he was in water and not on land. He began swimming. The others swam behind.

They rushed into the submarine. They had come out slowly, but zipped in at twice the speed.

Yadi and Diya sat down on the floor, panting. Diya looked through the wall and screamed. The five merlions pressed their faces against the wall, showing their big, pointy fangs. Diya crawled away from the wall, pulling Yadi with her.

'They are leaving,' said Jit. The creatures had turned away from the submarine.

'Good!' said Gulgul. 'There's nothing they can do now.'

But the merlions came back. They dashed towards the submarine.

They bashed and crashed against its wall. The submarine shook in the shock.

'They seem mad at us,' said Gulgul.

'Would you like it if your lunch ran away?' asked Jit.

'Breakfast, Papa,' Gulgul corrected him, 'Too early for lunch.'

BAM! The submarine shook again. WHAM! The merlions kept

attacking the submarine again and again.

'Won't they ever get tired?' asked Yadi.

'Won't the glass break?' asked Diya.

'It's the strongest glass in the world, Ma'am!' declared Piya. BRRRRRRROOOOOOOOOSH! The submarine moved upwards. The creatures swam away in alarm.

'It's unstuck!' Peter had a big smile now.

'Ha ha! The merlions helped lift the submarine from the sand,' laughed Megha.

'Thank you, Merlions!' said Gulgul.

'From bad things, good things can sometimes happen,' said Megha.

Gulgul, Girl Genius

'Let's keep going in a straight route,' Captain Piya told Peter. 'We will reach land soon.'

'Okay, Captain.'

The ship shot forward, leaving the merlions far behind.

'You know, Mamma, I have been thinking,' said Gulgul, 'Paru can fly, can't she?'

'Paru flies,' said Paru.

'Yes, of course, dear,' said Megha. 'She's a parrot, isn't she?'

'Suppose we send her out ahead? Ask her to spot land? She can look for land and come back and tell…'

'EEEEEEEEEEEEEEEEEEEEEE EEEEEEE!' screamed Megha, jumping out of her seat.

'What happened?' asked Jit in alarm.

Megha began screaming and dancing.

'EEEE! EEEEE! EEEE!'

Everybody stared at her.

Megha grabbed Gulgul, and kissed her on both cheeks.

'Mamma's darling! Clever girl! Ummmmmaaa! Genius Gulgul! Ummmmmaaa!'

'Thank you, Mamma,' said Gulgul, rubbing her cheek. 'But why? What? How?'

'Who? Where?' asked Paru.

'You see, dear,' said Megha, 'Mamma designs so many big things, that she forgets the little things she made. Sometimes the little things become very useful, too.'

'What's she saying, Papa?' asked Gulgul.

'I don't know, Gulgul. She talks like this sometimes.'

Megha ran over to the front of the ship.

'Captain Piya! Captain Piya!' she yelled in Piya's ear.

'Yes, I can hear, I am here, stop shouting please,' Piya rubbed her aching ear.

'Gulgul, send Paru here. You know Paru, Captain?' asked Megha.

Paru flew over to perch on Megha's shoulder.

'Yes, your daughter's robot pet parrot. I know her,' nodded Piya.

'I designed her, you know,' said Megha. 'I am an engineer.'

'Oh?' said Piya with respect.

'I forgot something. Something very important. When I designed her, I had a minimap app installed in her.'

'What does a mini app map do?'

'Minimap app,' corrected Megha. 'It's like Maps, but can't do everything Maps does. But it does one thing that's useful to us now.'

'What does it do?' asked Piya.

'Paru saves the location of each and every place she has been to. She must have the location of the water park saved. All we have to do is to ask her to fly there.'

'Great idea!' said Piya. 'She can

contact someone and give them our location.'

Megha frowned. Piya had not understood. But Peter understood.

'No, silly! I mean, Captain,' he laughed. 'We can ask her to fly there. Then we follow her to the water park.'

'Shut up, Peter,' said Piya. 'Great idea, Megha!'

'My daughter Gulgul's idea!' said Megha proudly.

'Peter, let's go to the surface,' said Piya. 'Then, open the hatch for Paro to fly out.'

'Paru,' corrected Megha.

Peter took the submarine upwards till it reached the surface of the sea. He pressed the hatch button.

'Gulgul darling?' Megha said, after she returned to her seat with Paru. 'Ask Paru to fly to the water park.'

'Okay, Mamma. Paru, fly to the water park, please. Don't fly too high or too fast, though.'

'Good thinking, Genius Girl,' said Megha.

'Don't fly too low, or too slow, too. Don't fly sideways or...'

'Okay, okay, that's enough!' said Megha.

Paru flew out of the hatch.

'Peter, follow the parut, I mean, parrot,' ordered the captain.

Peter made the submarine match

its speed with Paru, and follow her closely.

'Yay!' said Gulgul. 'We are on our way!'

Back to the Park

'Happy news, passengers!' said Captain Piya. 'We will soon reach the water park. Thanks to Gulgul and her mother here. Let's give them a big hand!'

Everybody clapped and cheered.

'Thank you very much, Megha and Gulgul,' said Diya.

'You saved us! It's such a big relief!' Yadi shook Gulgul's hand.

'Proud of you ladies,' said Jit.

'Including Paru,' said Gulgul.

'Her, too,' said Jit.

'I wish I had thought of it earlier,' said Megha. 'Silly me! Forgetful me!'

'Aw, Mamma, if you had thought of it earlier, we wouldn't have had fun at Octopus City,' said Gulgul. 'So, thank you for not remembering. Got to not only see a turtle, but stay on a turtle, too!'

'Ha ha! You're welcome, dear! Glad you had fun there.'

'Fun, yes,' said Jit. 'Except for the

salt water. Can still taste it. Grass and salt water!'

'Yuck!' Gulgul made a face. 'The fruits and nuts were yum, though.'

'Look, Mamma,' said Gulgul. 'The seabras again.'

She waved to the playful creatures in the sea. They swam alongside the submarine for some time, and then dived into the water.

'Bye, seabras! See y'all later! Beware of merlions!'

'I am connected now,' announced Maps suddenly.

'Where were you when we needed you?' asked Peter. 'We don't need you anymore. We have a parrot with a map app.'

'Don't be rude to Maps, Peter,' said Piya. 'These people will leave today with their parrot. We will have only Maps to help us in future.'

'We should ask Gulgul's mom to design a parrot for us. Then we will never be lost, with or without connection.'

'Good idea, Peter. I'll ask her right away.'

Megha promised to send them a parrot with a minimap app.

'Land ahead!' shouted Peter, after a while. The water park could be seen in the distance.

'Yay!' cheered everybody.

The submarine soon got docked, and the passengers stepped out. The Dev and Anand family stepped out first.

'Whew!' said Yadi. 'Safe and sound.'

'Thank the pilots, Yadi,' said Diya. 'Thank you, Pilots!'

'Thank you, Pilots,' chorused Yadi, Dev and Anand.

'Thank you, Captain Piya and Co-pilot Peter,' said Jit.

'Thank you,' said Megha and Gulgul.

'Thank you, really,' said Piya.

'Please remember to design a parrot for us,' said Peter.

'Will send you one soon,' said Megha.

'Bye,' said Gulgul.

'Bye-bye,' said Paru.

'Aaaaah!' Jit jumped on to the bed in their room in Sea-saw Gara. 'I'm happy to be back here. You ladies go and have fun. I think I will sleep here till you return. Glass submarines! Aquariums! I am tired of all those glass walls. Give me a proper room like this any day.'

'I am tired, too,' said Megha. 'I don't want to go on any more rides. Unless Gulgul wants to...?'

'No, Mamma. Let's go home. I miss my room.'

'Your messy room,' laughed Megha. 'Let's pack our bags, then.'

'Wake me up when ready.' Jit closed his eyes.

'You know, Papa...' said Gulgul. 'Next time, let's not go to a water place. No seas or beaches.' The three were now in a cab, on their way to Planet GR33N.

'No glass submarines or glass rooms, either,' said Jit.

'And let's always take Paru along,' said Megha.

'Yes,' said Jit. 'Good girl, Paru!'

'Thank you, Papaya!' said Paru.

'Don't call me Papaya!'